W9-CFV-578

Crack!

A hole appeared in the wall right over Shrew's fireplace. In its center was a black snout.

"Oh, no!" Shrew groaned.

"Oh, dear," said Mole. "I think I'm lost again."

There was a *thump*

and a **BUMP**

and a CR-R-ASH!

Mole rolled out onto the hearth.

Shrew shook her head.

"Mole," she said, "I think I'd better help you find a home."

Books by Jackie French Koller

Picture Books
Bouncing on the Bed
Nickommoh! A Thanksgiving Celebration
No Such Thing
One Monkey Too Many

Chapter Books
The Dragonling *books*
The Mole and Shrew *series*
The Promise

Novels: Middle-Grade & Up
If I Had One Wish
The Last Voyage of the Misty Day
Nothing to Fear
The Primrose Way

Novels: Young Adult
The Falcon
A Place to Call Home

MOle AND Shrew Are Two

#1

by Jackie French Koller
illustrated by Anne Reas

A STEPPING STONE BOOK™
Random House New York

To Kerri, whose smiles are like sunshine

Text copyright © 2000 by Jackie French Koller
Illustrations copyright © 2000 by Anne Reas
All rights reserved under International and Pan-American Copyright
Conventions. Published in the United States by Random House, Inc.,
New York, and simultaneously in Canada by Random House of Canada
Limited, Toronto.

www.randomhouse.com/kids

Library of Congress Cataloging-in-Publication Data
Koller, Jackie French.
Mole and Shrew are two / by Jackie French Koller ;
illustrated by Anne Reas.
p. cm. — "A Stepping Stone book."
Summary: Shrew proves to be a good friend to Mole in various
situations, including finding a new house and attending a fancy ball.
ISBN 0-375-80690-3 (pbk.) — ISBN 0-375-90690-8 (lib. bdg.)
[1. Moles (Animals)—Fiction. 2. Shrews—Fiction. 3. Friendship—Fiction.]
I. Reas, Anne, ill. II. Title.
PZ7.K833 Mom   2000   [E]—dc21   00-026024

Printed in the United States of America   October 2000   10 9 8 7 6 5 4 3 2 1

Random House, Inc. New York, Toronto, London, Sydney, Auckland
RANDOM HOUSE and colophon are registered trademarks and A STEPPING STONE BOOK
and colophon are trademarks of Random House, Inc.

☀ Contents ☀

1

Mole Drops In

Shrew stretched and yawned. Golden sunshine streamed in through her window. A lark sang merrily on a branch just outside.

"Oh, my," said Shrew. "It looks like a lovely day."

Shrew slipped into her robe and scuffies and padded into the bathroom. She took her toothbrush out of the holder and opened the door to her medicine cabinet. She blinked, rubbed her eyes, and then slammed the cabinet shut.

1

"There's a face in my cabinet!" she screamed.

"Help!" came a muffled cry.

Shrew trembled. "Wh-who said that?" she asked.

"Me," said a voice.

"Me who?" asked Shrew.

"Me...Mole," said the voice.

"Why are you in my cabinet?" asked Shrew.

"I'm not quite sure," said Mole, sounding very forlorn.

Shrew opened the cabinet just far enough to see Mole's frightened eyes.

"What's wrong?" she asked.

"I'm lost," said Mole.

"I should say so!" cried Shrew.

"Well, go ahead, then," said Mole.

"Go ahead and what?" asked Shrew.

"Go ahead and say so," said Mole.

"I just did," said Shrew.

"Oh." Mole sighed. "I really *must* listen more carefully."

Shrew opened the cabinet wider. "You appear to be stuck," she said.

"I am," said Mole, "but I think I can manage. May I drop in?"

"Do I have a choice?" asked Shrew.

"I'm afraid not," said Mole, "unless you *like* having a face in your medicine cabinet."

Shrew sighed. "Well, come ahead, then."

Mole wiggled and squirmed, and great piles of dirt fell out around him.

"You're making quite a mess," snapped Shrew.

"I'm sorry," said Mole, "but I burrowed my way in, you see, and burrowing *is* a messy business."

Suddenly, Mole slid out, snout first, into

the washbasin. And there he stayed.

"Are you going to come out from there?" asked Shrew.

"My thnout ith thtuck in the dwain," said Mole.

"Well!" exclaimed Shrew. "That is *most* inconvenient."

"Perhapth if you pulled on my legth?" said Mole.

"Oh, all right," huffed Shrew.

She gave one hard tug. Out popped Mole!

"Now," said Shrew, "kindly explain *how* you came to be in my cabinet."

"Well," said Mole, "it's a long story."

Shrew crossed her arms and waited.

2

Mole's Tale

"It all began with my aunt Phoebe," said Mole.

"Your aunt Phoebe?" said Shrew.

"Yes," Mole went on. "She came to visit, and I tried to make her comfortable."

"But you couldn't?" Shrew asked.

"I could," said Mole. "I could indeed. I made her so comfortable that she never went home. She moved into my den. Then she invited her nephew Fred and his family to move in. Fred has five children. They took over the parlor."

"Oh, my," said Shrew.

"Then came poor old Uncle Mack. I gave him my room."

"But where did *you* go?" asked Shrew.

"I put a cot in the kitchen," said Mole, "that is, until Cousin Louie arrived with his soccer team."

"Soccer team!" exclaimed Shrew.

"So I tried the bathroom," Mole continued, "but there was an awful lot of traffic in and out."

"I should imagine," said Shrew.

"Yes, you should," said Mole. "Imagining is fun."

"No," said Shrew. "I mean, I *do* imagine there was a lot of traffic."

"Oh, yes, there was" said Mole, "and

that's why I'm here."

"You're looking for another bathroom?" said Shrew.

"No," said Mole. "I'm looking for another home." He peeked out of the bathroom door. "This is a very nice home," he said.

"Yes," said Shrew sharply, "this is *my* home."

"Oh," said Mole. "Well, then, this is a nice bathroom. A *very* nice bathroom."

"I think," said Shrew firmly, "that you should leave."

"All right," said Mole with a sigh. He started to climb back up into the wash-basin.

"Not that way!" cried Shrew. "This way." She showed Mole to the door.

"Well, good-bye," said Mole.

"Good-bye," said Shrew. *"And good riddance,"* she added as soon as the door closed behind Mole.

Shrew went into *her* bedroom and got dressed. Then she made herself a hot cup of tea. She sat down in *her* sitting room to drink it.

Crack!

A hole appeared in the wall right over Shrew's fireplace. In its center was a black snout.

"Oh, no!" Shrew groaned.

"Oh, dear," said Mole. "I think I'm lost again."

There was a *thump* and a **BUMP** and a CR-R-ASH!

Mole rolled out onto the hearth.
Shrew shook her head.

"Mole," she said, "I think I'd better help you find a home."

☀ 3 ☀

House Hunting

After a light breakfast of tea and toast, Shrew took Mole house hunting. They went to the old cave where Badger used to live.

Mole shook his head. "Too big," he said.

Next, Shrew took him to Squirrel's abandoned nest in a pine tree.

"Too drafty," said Mole.

She took him to Snake's old crack in a rock.

"Too hard," said Mole.

She took him home for lunch.

"Just right!" said Mole.

"Mole," said Shrew, "this is *my* house."

"Oh," said Mole.

After lunch, Shrew showed Mole Tree Toad's old home.

"Too small," said Mole.

And Otter's abandoned den.

"Too damp," said Mole.

And Owl's empty nest.

"Too *scary*," said Mole.

It was growing dark.

"Mole," said Shrew, "you are very hard to please."

Just then, Mole spied something.

"What is that?" he asked.

"Nothing," said Shrew.

"It looks like a house," said Mole.

"I doubt it," said Shrew.

"It is!" cried Mole. "I believe it's an abandoned chipmunk den."

"It's too *close*," muttered Shrew.

"What did you say, Shrew?"

"Nothing," muttered Shrew.

"Why, it's perfect!" shouted Mole. "And look, Shrew. Your home is right next door. We'll be neighbors!"

Shrew was silent.

* 4 *
Neighbors

Shrew got up and started breakfast. She put on a pot of tea and poured some batter into a skillet. Just then, a knock came on the door. Shrew hurried to answer it.

"Good morning, neighbor!" cried Mole. "I wonder if I might borrow your hedge trimmers."

"I suppose so," said Shrew. "They're in the potting shed."

"Thank you," said Mole. He sniffed the

air. "Mmmm," he said, "something smells very good."

"Hotcakes," said Shrew.

"Oh," said Mole, licking his lips. "I do love hotcakes."

Shrew sighed.

"Mole," she said, "would you like some breakfast?"

"Why, Shrew," said Mole, "how kind of you to ask."

Later, when Shrew was fixing lunch, another knock came on the door.

"Shrew," said Mole, "may I borrow a bucket?"

"Yes, go right ahead," said Shrew. She started to close the door, but Mole poked his snout in.

"Do I smell soup?" he asked.

Shrew nodded slowly.

"I would make some soup," said Mole wistfully, "if only I could find my pot."

Shrew sighed again. "Mole," she said, "won't you stay for lunch?"

That evening, Shrew had no sooner started to fix dinner when she heard another knock.

"Enough is enough!" she said, untying her apron and flinging it aside. "Neighbors or not, I'm not giving that freeloader one more meal!"

She stomped over to the door and pulled it open.

"Good evening, Shrew," said Mole. He handed her a bucket filled with flowers.

"What's this?" asked Shrew.

"Your bucket," said Mole. "Good neighbors never return things empty. And here are your trimmers. They were a little dull, so I took the liberty of sharpening them."

"Why…thank you, Mole," said Shrew.

Mole blushed. "It was the least I could do," he said. "Oh, and Shrew?"

"Yes, Mole?" Shrew asked warily.

"Well, it's almost dinnertime," said Mole, "and I was wondering…that is…if you wouldn't mind…"

Shrew sighed.

"*Yes*, Mole?" she snapped.

Mole cleared his throat. "The thing is…" he said, "I've prepared a special dinner…to celebrate my new home…"

Shrew's eyes widened.

"And I was wondering," Mole added quickly, "would you join me?"

Shrew blinked in surprise. Then she smiled.

"Why, Mole," she said, "I should be delighted."

"Yes, you should," said Mole, blushing again. "I'm a very good cook."

Shrew laughed.

"I'm sure you are, Mole," she said, "and I'm beginning to think you're going to be a very good neighbor, too."

☀5☀

An Invitation

It was a lovely spring day.

"I think I'll go out for a stroll," Mole said to himself.

He picked up his walking stick and headed out the door. He walked up the lane. Shrew was watering the flowers around her mailbox.

"Good day, Shrew," said Mole. "Isn't this weather fine?"

"It certainly is," said Shrew. "How are

you enjoying your new home, Mole?"

"Oh, very well," said Mole, "very well indeed."

Just then, the postman came down the hill with his big leather sack over his shoulder. He stopped and handed Shrew an envelope. It was blue, with fancy silver writing.

"Oh!" cried Shrew. "It's here!"

"Of course it's here," said Mole. "The mail comes every day."

"Not the mail," said Shrew, "my invitation to the ball!"

"The ball?" said Mole. "What ball?"

"The ball at Mouse Manor," said Shrew. "It is *the* social event of the year. *Everybody* who's *anybody* is invited."

Shrew hugged her invitation happily. "I must go call and accept," she said. Then she dashed up her walk and into her house.

Mole stared after her. "Everybody who is *anybody*?" he repeated.

Mole turned and hurried home. He got there just as the postman was walking away. Mole looked into his mailbox.

It was empty.

"Wait!" cried Mole, running after the postman. "Please wait!"

The postman stopped and waited for Mole to catch up.

"Is there a blue envelope with silver writing for *me?*" Mole asked.

The postman looked through his fat pack of blue envelopes.

"Nope," he said. "No blue envelope for Mole."

"Oh, dear," said Mole. He turned away and walked slowly home.

Mole looked at himself in his front hall mirror.

"Hello, Mole," he said.

Nobody answered.

"Oh, dear," said Mole.

He yelled his name out the front door.

Nobody came.

He called louder.

Still nobody came.

Mole rushed outside and ran all the way to Shrew's house. He banged on her door.

"Shrew," he cried breathlessly, "may I use your phone?"

"Why, of course," said Shrew. "Is something wrong?"

"I'm afraid so," said Mole.

He dialed his own number.

"Oh, dear, oh, dear," he mumbled.

"Whatever is the matter?" asked Shrew.

"I just called myself up," said Mole, "and *nobody* answered!"

Shrew looked at him oddly. "So?" she said.

"Don't you see?" said Mole. "I'm *nobody*."

Shrew took the phone out of Mole's hand.

"Mole," she said, "whatever are you talking about?"

"I didn't get an invitation to the ball," said Mole, "so I can't be *anybody*, and I spoke to myself in the mirror and nobody answered, then I called myself in the yard and nobody came, and now nobody answered my phone! Oh, dear, oh, dear." He put his head between his hands and heaved a great sigh.

Shrew smiled and gently patted Mole's shoulder.

"Don't be silly, Mole," she said. "Of course you are somebody. You didn't get an invitation to the ball because you've just moved into the neighborhood. Mouse hasn't met you yet. You shall go to the ball as *my* guest."

"Really?" said Mole.

"Really," said Shrew.

"Oh, thank you, thank you," said Mole.

Mole's Tail

Mole's phone rang early one morning. It was Shrew.

"Don't forget," she said. "Tonight is the ball!"

"How could I forget?" said Mole. "I can hardly wait."

"Pick me up at eight," said Shrew, "and remember to wear a black tie and tails."

Mole hung up the phone and started singing a happy little song to himself.

"Tonight at eight.

I won't be late.

Black tie and tails.

Black tie and..."

Suddenly, he stopped singing. "Tails?" he said out loud. "Tails?"

Mole looked forlornly over his shoulder. He had only one tail, and it was a short, stubby thing at that.

"Oh, dear," he moaned. "I simply *must* find some suitable tails by eight o'clock. But where?"

Mole dashed out of his house and hurried up the lane, looking left and right. Before long, he heard a hearty *slap, slap, slap*. It was Beaver working on a new dam down at the pond.

"Beaver has a wonderful tail," said Mole

to himself. "Oh, yes, a magnificent tail!" He hurried down to the water's edge.

"Pardon me," he said. "I'm sorry to interrupt, but…"

Beaver stopped working and looked at Mole. "Yes?" he said.

"Well," said Mole, "it's just that…I wondered if I might borrow your tail."

"My tail!" Beaver's eyes nearly popped out of his head. "Are you *mad?*" he said gruffly.

"Mad?" repeated Mole. "Oh, no, not at all. I'm in a very good mood actually. At least I *was* until this whole tail business came up."

"You *are* mad," said Beaver with a snort.

"No, I'm not. Really, I'm not!" Mole protested.

But it was too late. Beaver had plunged under the water and disappeared.

"Humph," said Mole. "Perhaps I was too direct."

"Got a problem?" someone asked.

Mole turned and saw Lizard sunning herself on a nearby rock. He couldn't help but admire her sleek, colorful tail.

"I say, is something wrong?" Lizard repeated.

"Oh," said Mole, "not really. It's just that my tail is so puny. It won't do at all, and besides I only have one."

32

"How many does a body need?" asked Lizard. "One has always served me well enough."

"Well, I'm not sure," said Mole. "Two at least, maybe more. It's Mouse's ball, you see, and Shrew didn't say."

Lizard shook her head. "Sounds like a bunch of poppycock to me," she said, "but if it means that much to you, I'll give you mine."

Mole was astonished. "Do you mean it?" he cried.

"Of course I mean it," said Lizard. "Wouldn't say it if I didn't." And with a sudden *snap*, she broke her tail free and handed it to Mole.

"My!" said Mole. "Doesn't that sting?"

"Just a bit," said Lizard, "but don't worry. I'll grow a new one in no time."

"Really?" said Mole. He thought for a moment. "How *soon* could you grow another one?" he asked.

"When do you need it?" asked Lizard.

"Tonight," said Mole.

"Not *that* soon," said Lizard.

"Oh," said Mole. "Well, thank you just the same." He held up Lizard's tail and admired it. "You've been *most* kind," he added. Then he started to walk away.

"Wait," said Lizard.

Mole turned back.

Lizard pointed to the sky. "Isn't that a kite up there?" she said.

"Indeed it is," said Mole.

"And doesn't a kite have a tail?" asked Lizard.

"Indeed it *does*," said Mole. "Oh, thank you *again*, Lizard. You've been such a big help."

Mole ran off in the direction of the kite. He found the kite attached to a string, which was attached to a very small frog.

"Pardon me," said Mole, "but I wondered if I might borrow your kite tail."

Frog looked up at Mole with large eyes. "But my kite won't fly without it," he said.

"I only need it for tonight," said Mole, "and I'll take good care of it. I wouldn't ask if it weren't *very* important."

Frog hung his head. "Well, all right," he

said, "if it's *very* important."

Frog pulled his kite in and gave the tail to Mole.

"Thank you," said Mole. "I'll have it back first thing in the morning. I promise." He tucked the kite tail under his arm along with Lizard's. "I do hope two is enough," he mumbled. "It would be nice to have one more, just to be safe."

"One more what?" someone asked in a high, thin voice.

Mole looked up to see Silkworm perched on a branch overhead.

"One more tail," said Mole. "I'm in need of tails."

"Sit down, then," said Silkworm, "and I'll spin you one. I'm a great spinner of tales."

Mole sat down. Silkworm began to spin the most wondrous tale of kings and queens and sailing ships, and far-off castles by the sea. All the while she talked, she danced and twirled. When she was done, she handed Mole a tail of shining silk.

"It's beautiful," cried Mole. He tucked this treasure under his arm with the others, turned around, and started for home. "Thank you. Thank you all!" he called out as he passed each of his new friends. "Someday I'll return the favor. You'll see."

☀ 7 ☀

Mole's Grand Entrance

It was getting late. Mole washed and dressed in his dapper plaid suit. He wound his beautiful silk tail around his head like a turban. He tied the kite tail around his waist like a belt. He hung Lizard's tail from the belt like a saber. Then he tied his black tie around his neck.

"Oh, my," he said, admiring himself in the mirror. "I do look fine."

BONG BONG BONG BONG BONG BONG BONG BONG went Mole's clock.

"Dear me!" he cried. "Shrew will never forgive me if we're late!"

He rushed over and got to Shrew's door just as she was coming out. When Shrew saw him, her eyes grew wide and her mouth dropped open.

"I knew I looked fine," said Mole, "but I didn't think you'd be speechless."

Shrew could only shake her head. "B-but, Mole," she stammered.

"No time to chat now," said Mole. "We're running late!"

When Mole and Shrew arrived at Mouse Manor, the butler was speechless, too. Mole beamed with pride. He ushered Shrew down the stairs and into the Grand Ballroom.

A sudden hush fell over the crowd.

"Mercy!" cried Mouse.

Mole looked around. All the male guests were dressed in penguin suits.

"You didn't tell me it was a costume ball," Mole whispered to Shrew. "You said to wear tails."

"Those aren't costumes," whispered Shrew. "They are tuxedos. They are called tails, for short. I'm sorry. I thought you knew."

Suddenly, Mole felt very foolish. The other guests were starting to snicker and laugh. "Excuse me," he said, bowing to Mouse. "I just remembered. It's my bowling night."

Then he dashed out of the house as fast as he could.

Mole sat down on a log. He felt awful,

simply awful. What a fool he'd made of himself. How would he ever face his neighbors again?

"May I sit down, too?"

Mole looked up. It was Shrew.

"You'll dirty your beautiful gown," he said.

"I don't care," said Shrew. She sat down next to Mole.

"You're missing the ball," said Mole.

"It was a very stuffy ball anyway," said Shrew. "I'd rather be with you."

"You're a good friend," said Mole.

"So are you," said Shrew. "In fact, I think we should have a ball of our own—a Good Friends Ball."

"Oh," said Mole, "that's a wonderful idea! Do you think we could invite Lizard and Frog and Silkworm?"

"Of course we can," said Shrew. "We'll invite all of our friends and we'll make sure nobody is left out."

Mole was quiet.

"Is something wrong, Mole?" asked Shrew.

"Well," said Mole, "couldn't we invite Nobody, too? I hate to see anyone left out."

Shrew laughed. "Of course, dear Mole," she said. "I shall put Nobody at the top of our list!"

8

The Good Friends Ball

Mole and Shrew were busy all week.

They wrote out invitations and gave them to the postman. They scrubbed Mole's house till it sparkled. They shopped and cooked and baked. They gathered flowers from Shrew's garden. They hung streamers and blew up balloons. The big day finally arrived!

"This is going to be the best ball ever," said Mole.

"Just wait until everyone sees these decorations," said Shrew.

"And tastes the food," added Mole. The food was Mole's favorite part. He had made the tarts himself.

"The guests will be arriving soon," said Shrew. "I'd better run home and change."

Mole changed, too, into his best jacket and his polka-dot tie.

When Shrew came back, they set about lighting the candles and lanterns.

"Ahh," said Shrew when everything was ready. "It's like a fairyland, Mole."

"And you look like the fairy princess," said Mole.

Shrew blushed. "Why, thank you, Mole. I must say you are looking rather handsome yourself."

DING DONG went Mole's doorbell.

"They're here!" cried Mole.

He ran to open the door. Outside stood a great, happy throng.

"Come in! Come in!" cried Mole.

Mole and Shrew's friends started filing in. Rabbit and Hare made quite a handsome pair. Silkworm had invited Caterpillar, who was resplendent in his fur coat. Frog came in with Toad, and Fox was with Coyote. Lizard, sporting a lovely new tail, came with Salamander.

Two by two the couples came through the door until the house was bursting with happy guests. After the last couple, Mole poked his head outside. He looked left and right, then left and right again.

"Is something wrong?" asked Squirrel, who had been the last to arrive.

"I don't see Nobody," said Mole.

Squirrel looked around the room. "Don't worry," she said. "We're all in, so nobody should be left out."

Mole frowned. "Well, *that's* rude," he said.

Squirrel looked at him oddly and walked away. Mole took one last look outside, then slowly shut the door. He walked over to get some punch.

"Everything looks just lovely," said Rabbit.

"Oh, thank you," Mole answered quietly.

"Is something wrong?" asked Rabbit.

"I don't see Nobody," said Mole.

"You mean you don't see *anybody*," Rabbit corrected him.

"No, that's not what I mean at all," said Mole. "I *do* see anybody. I see anybody and everybody, but I don't see Nobody."

Rabbit shook his head. "I'm afraid I don't understand," he said.

"Oh, never mind," said Mole. He walked away, mumbling to himself.

"What's that you said?" asked Fox.

"I said I'm surprised," said Mole. "I really expected Nobody to come."

"Why would you think that?" asked Fox. "Everybody likes you, Mole."

Mole thought for a moment. "If everybody came because everybody likes me," he said, "then that must mean Nobody doesn't like me."

"Precisely," said Fox.

"Oh, dear," said Mole.

Suddenly, the doorbell rang again.

"Oh," cried Mole. "I'll bet that's Nobody now." He hurried away, leaving Fox scratching his head.

DING DONG went the bell again.

"I'm coming!" cried Mole. He reached the door and pulled it open. There stood Beaver.

"Sorry I'm late," said Beaver. "Had to brush my teeth. Takes me a bit longer than most, you know."

"No problem," said Mole quietly. "Come right in."

Beaver joined the other guests.

Mole stood peering out into the night. Shrew came up behind him.

"Mole," she said, "are you all right? Everybody is worried about you."

Mole sighed. "That's because everybody likes me," he said.

"And what's wrong with that?" asked Shrew.

"Nothing," said Mole. "It's just that

Nobody *doesn't* like me."

Shrew stared at Mole wonderingly.

"You see," said Mole, "Fox told me that everybody came because everybody likes me and Nobody didn't come because Nobody doesn't like me. And then the doorbell rang again and I thought maybe it was Nobody. But it wasn't. It was just Beaver."

Shrew smiled. "Ah," she said. "Now I see. But you're wrong, Mole. I have a surprise for you."

"What is it?" asked Mole.

Shrew looked over at Beaver.

"Beaver," she said, "would you kindly tell Mole who you came with tonight?"

"Nobody," said Beaver.

Mole's eyes lit up.

"You see," said Shrew, "Nobody *did*

come. Are you happy now, Mole?"

"Oh, yes!" Mole beamed. "Very happy."

"Good," said Shrew. "Then would you care to take a turn on the dance floor?"

"Do we have to take turns?" asked Mole. "I was rather hoping we could dance together."

Shrew grinned. "I was rather hoping the same thing, Mole," she said.

She took Mole's arm and steered him toward the dance floor. The band struck up a lively tune and all the guests started to rock-and-roll. Right in the middle of the crowd, shaking and shimmying and having a ball, was Beaver.

Mole smiled. "Isn't it nice to see that Nobody is having a good time?" he whispered in Shrew's ear.

"Indeed," Shrew said with a merry little

laugh. "I'll bet we're the first folks ever to throw a party where *Nobody* has a good time and *everybody* has a ball!"

Want to spend more time with Mole and Shrew?

Celebrate five holidays with these two funny friends and find out:

1) how to make a fresh tart for the new year
2) if hunting Easter eggs is dangerous
3) what to do if you have a fight with your best friend about Fourth of July plans
4) how to survive a Thanksgiving disaster
5) where to find a "fur" tree

in:

Mole and Shrew All Year Through

Jackie French Koller

is the mother of three grown children, the wife of a wonderful man named George, and the author of over two dozen books for children and young adults. She lives on a mountaintop in western Massachusetts, where she shares her studio with her doll, Susie, her dogs, Sara and Cassie; hundreds of books; a cranky computer; piles of papers; assorted dust bunnies; and all of the creatures of her imagination, including her old and dear friends Mole and Shrew.